Bob Stegner grew up on  some wonderful places teacher, a published singe his own school in Alaska, worked for an educational technology company, and has been a technology specialist in the northwestern part of the U. S. as well as teaching overseas in Vienna, Austria and Warsaw, Poland. He's also worked in a department store and a ski area in Colorado where he was a "ski bumb" for a couple of years. Now, he's back in the northwest working hard on his writing and enjoying the outdoors. His work consists of novels, short stories and poetry.

Visit Bob's writer's blog to keep up with what he's doing as an author: http://bobstegner.blogspot.com/

Wheatgrass
An Irish Fantasy

Bob Stegner

CreateSpace Independent Publishing Platform; 1 edition (November 20, 2013)

ISBN-10: 1494236745
ISBN-13: 978-1494236748

Copyright © Bob Stegner 2013

This book is dedicated to one of my dearest friends.

This story takes place in eastern, old Ireland and across the Irish Sea in Wales. It is a fanciful tale about Eire and her incredible seabird, Wheatgrass. It's a story that has a castle, a village named Blackwater and a very dangerous wizard named Dalbhach and his raven, Rocas. It has happiness and sadness, and fear, and hope and love, and the challenge of living life as you wish...

1

On the eastern coast of Ireland long ago near the village of Blackwater, a beautiful young lass named Eire (Ayreh) was out on a warm, sunny autumn day. She often went for walks and was known by almost everyone in the village as a very curious, joyful young girl. She had a smile that could light up the morning and laughed and talked easily with those that she knew. On this particular day, her walk had taken her near the Irish Sea. She ran and jumped and reveled in the fresh salt breeze as it blew lightly through her golden-brown hair. She noticed the plants growing abundantly, the birds floating and gliding in the sky, and the seawater as it crashed up against the rocks at the water's edge spraying foam upon the land. On her way, she found a rare patch of wild Irish wheat and bent down to touch it and take in its earthy, herbal aromas. As she did so, she heard a soft, high sound. It was not a sound that she had heard often. It seemed, as she moved closer to it, that it was a young sound, possibly the sound of a tiny bird.

She spread the blades of wheat with her fingers, gazing and searching in different directions, following the noise with her eyes. She knew she was close. Eire found the young one. It was a bird that she recognized - a seabird. It was the type of bird that she had seen many times flying near her home and had noticed them soaring far out across the Irish Sea. It also reminded Eire of her friend on the other side of the sea in the village of Trefin in Wales. Her name was Devyn, and she loved to draw pictures of birds. Eire had grown up with Devyn, but when they were both much younger, Devyn had left Blackwater with her parents. Though it had been difficult, Eire and Devyn had stayed in contact, sharing messages that had been carried on sailing vessels that crossed the Irish Sea. Devyn had told her about the beauty of her home and had also sent drawings of birds that were similar to this little one. Eire wondered if these birds actually flew clear across the sea.

She placed the young bird in her hands and softly spoke to it. The tiny creature peeped and tilted its head. She marveled at the softness of the down and felt sorry for it's plight. It was obvious that it was there in the grass because of some event beyond its control. Eire wondered where the baby's mother was. If she left it there, he would surely die. She stood and walked, carrying the young bird back to her home. She knew that she would have to raise it with love and care. As she walked, she named the bird Wheatgrass.

***

Several months passed, and Wheatgrass had survived and grown strong. He had not only survived, but Eire was able to release him into the wild. He had become a very powerful bird for his size and flew great distances, but he always returned to her. He was also extremely intelligent and seemed to understand Erie's words and sense her feelings. He even appeared to know when she needed him. They were very close.

Eire discovered how truly amazing Wheatgrass was one day when he was tilting his head, giving her the impression that he was listening to her very intently. So, on a lark, Eire asked Wheatgrass to take a note to her family to tell them she was going to be awhile gathering peat for their cooking fire. She would be home a little later than expected.

She placed the note in front of Wheatgrass, and he clawed it and flew away. Eire stood with a surprised look on her face, gazing in wonder as he flew off toward their home.

She continued to gather peat, thinking it was just a coincidence, but only a short while later, Wheatgrass landed next to her with another note in his claw. It was from Erie's mother. Her mother told her what Wheatgrass had done and that he had seemed to want to take something back to her, so she sent this note. Eire simply looked at Wheatgrass in amazement. He tilted his head as if questioning what she might ask of him next.

2

Two years passed, and Eire was now a young woman. She was of an age to be married but hadn't found the man of her dreams, yet she was happy and content. She loved her family, her friends, and Wheatgrass, who continually astounded her with his cleverness. Her family and the people in her village marveled at what he could do as well. The two of them had become an important part of the everyday life of Blackwater.

Eire and Devyn could now write back and forth whenever they wished because of Wheatgrass. His ability to fly long distances allowed him to easily migrate across the entire width of the Irish Sea to Wales in about two hours. With a sailing ship, it could take much longer. She didn't want Wheatgrass to have to do this too often, but he seemed to enjoy the journeys, and she loved hearing from her friend more frequently than the ships could bring the notes and drawings from her. Wheatgrass was becoming known on both sides of the sea.

One afternoon, Eire heard of a festival that was to be held in the village. A wizard with great powers was performing. His name was Dalbhach (DUL vakh). He lived high on a hill in Blackwater Castle about a day's walk from the village. He had lived there as long as anyone could remember. He never seemed to age and was a very tall, handsome, ominous figure. As the name of his castle suggested, his eyes were deep black pools, and his hair thick and dark as a moonless night. He was a powerful figure.

The people of Blackwater all knew of him, and they knew that no one should ever make Dalbhach angry. He had a reputation of making life very unpleasant for anyone who crossed him. He also had an extremely large raven that lived with him, whose demeanor was disturbing as well. His name was Rocas.

Even though Dalbhach and Rocas had very questionable reputations, it was still a big event in the life of the villagers to have such a celebration take place. Many people were there, and Eire was one of them.

Dalbhach had performed many wondrous feats that day, and everyone in the village was applauding and enjoying the performance. Rocas was even involved, as he changed form in the sky and flew swiftly through the crowd speaking to them in ways that everyone could understand. It was something to behold.

After completing the performance, Eire was about to leave when Dalbhach appeared next to her, his eyes piercing into her. She felt him before she actually saw him. He spoke to her, and she was immediately mesmerized. She felt as if she could listen to him for hours. His knowledge of the world and of life was something that she had never experienced. She could hardly leave him to go home, but finally managed to get away to be with her family.

***

In the afternoon of the next day at Eire's cottage, there was a knock at the door. Just before Eire walked to the door to see who it was, she heard a scratching at the window near her bed. She glanced over and saw Wheatgrass. She quickly walked over and opened the window. She hadn't seen her friend for about a month. He seemed agitated and was acting in a way that made Eire feel very uncomfortable. She had to go to the door, though, and needed to leave Wheatgrass on the windowsill for a moment. She opened the door and standing there was the large, commanding figure of Dalbhach with a strange smile on his face. Eire was immediately taken by him, just as she had been the day before, and she invited him in. As he entered the cottage, though, Wheatgrass flew from the window where he was perched, landed on Dalbhach's shoulder and pecked his neck making him bleed. Eire couldn't believe what she'd seen. She grabbed Wheatgrass with both hands, threw him into the air outside the house, and closed the window by her bed, keeping Wheatgrass outside.

Eire apologized to Dalbhach, but upon looking at him again, it didn't even seem as if he had been injured. He simply dismissed it. He spent the afternoon and evening with Eire and her family. Everyone was very impressed with him, and before the evening was over, he had asked for Eire's hand in marriage and everyone was very excited and happy, especially Eire.

As the plans were being made, a storm from the sea had moved in. The sky was dark and rain was pelting the small cottage. Outside in the rain, perched on a branch next to a window of the cottage looking in on the warm setting was Wheatgrass. Water was dripping from his feathers and beak; his head tilting back and forth, and his eyes focused on Eire.

3

The day of the wedding the entire village came out. Eire and her family were important members of the Blackwater community and loved by all of the people who lived there. Even though it was a beautiful day, Dalbhach had insisted that the ceremony take place in the large Abbey near Blackwater and was adamant that all of the doors and windows remain closed. He made the excuse that he didn't want to have to worry about a sudden change in weather that everyone knew could occur at any time in Ireland.

The wedding was beautiful and very festive, and the bride and groom and the raven, Rocas, were to leave for Blackwater Castle directly after the wedding in an extravagant carriage pulled by two large, strong ebony horses with long manes and tales like flowing water. The villagers gathered round and were giving the couple their best wishes when Eire looked into the sky and saw a small dot getting larger as it dove toward them. It didn't take Eire long to recognize that it was Wheatgrass. She hadn't seen him since the afternoon when she had agreed to marry Dalbhach.

She couldn't believe what was happening. Why was Wheatgrass diving down toward them at such speeds? As she was looking up, Dalbhach noticed and raised his eyes to the sky as well. He immediately saw Wheatgrass and lowered his gaze to whisper something inaudibly to Rocas. Rocas took off like a shot and accelerated toward Wheatgrass.

Eire yelled at Wheatgrass to worn him, but the birds soon collided in the air. Wheatgrass was much smaller than Rocas and lost the battle very quickly. Eire screamed in terror as she watched Wheatgrass fall to the earth in the tall grass. She quickly leapt out of the cart and started running toward where she thought Wheatgrass was, but just as she did this, Dalbhach's voice boomed out a phrase that no one understood. Eire collapsed on the spot. Dalbhach got out of the cart, walked over, picked her up in his great arms and carried her back to the carriage. Her family and friends gathered around to help, but just as they did, Eire awoke and seemed fine. Dalbhach waved off their concerns, and the crowd couldn't believe it, but Eire no longer seemed worried at all. Rocas landed and sat next to her. The carriage with the couple and the dark raven moved off into the distance toward Blackwater Castle.

The family and most of the villagers couldn't believe what had happened. After Eire left, they did their best to try to find Wheatgrass, but they were not successful. It was extremely difficult to know exactly where he might have landed in the tall grass. They couldn't hear or see him. They knew he was gone. The day that had started with such excitement and joy had ended with a dark veil that seemed as if it could never be lifted.

The villagers could not believe the sadness that they felt. No one, including Eire's family, could believe what had taken place. Eire had just wed a man whom she had known for less than a few days, and the family and villagers had approved. Why? To add to this, the incredible Wheatgrass lay somewhere near the village, either dying or dead, and no one dared challenge what had happened. The family and villagers were all very fearful of Dalbhach and Rocas. Life would never be the same in Blackwater.

***

Just as the villagers had seemed to come to their senses, so too had Eire. When she and Dalbhach reached the castle, she had begun to wonder why she was there and how she had come to be with him. It had happened so quickly, and after the first day or so of being her husband, he had changed and seemed less and less and less interested in her. Also, her memory of what had happened to Wheatgrass returned, and utter sadness and despair took the place of the complete ecstasy that she had felt only a few days before.

She began to question Dalbhach about what had happened and if he had done something to her family and to her that made them agree to the wedding. He rejected her questions and wouldn't even respond. This made Eire even more sad and angry. She missed her family and continually thought about the death of Wheatgrass.

***

One day, Eire was on one of her walks, and she decided to go home for a visit. She was so miserable and lonely. She hadn't even seen Dalbhach for days. He didn't seem to care, didn't touch her, talk to her, or spend any time with her, and Rocas had been watching her constantly no matter where she was or what she was doing.

However, Rocas wasn't around at the moment. This might be her only chance to leave to see her family. Without looking back, she started walking toward home. She knew it would take about a day, but she had packed extra food that morning for her walk, and she was determined.

The walk felt good. The air was crisp and the sun was shining. She knew that she was making good time and would be there soon. She felt better than she had in days, although her sadness about Wheatgrass still followed her wherever she went.

She had just climbed the last rise and was looking down on the village of Blackwater when she heard the raucous caw of Rocas. Her heart started pounding, and she turned quickly and saw Dalbhach walking toward her with Rocas on his shoulder. Rocas was screaming, and Dalbhach had an extremely angry look on his face; his eyes seemed to penetrate her very soul. Eire fell to the ground and darkness surrounded her. She dreamed of soaring above the earth, carried in muscular arms. She was laid down upon a soft bed as rays of light faded and dimmed, and her dream weakened and disappeared. She slept a very difficult sleep.

4

The news of what had happened at Eire's wedding had finally reached Devyn in Trefin. Eire's family had written to her. She was saddened and distraught from what she heard. Not only had she lost contact with her dear friend, but Eire's wonderful bird, Wheatgrass, had been killed. It was almost more that she could bear.

Devyn had many friends in the village of Trefin, one of which was an old fisherman's son named Sean. He too was saddened, as he had become used to watching for Wheatgrass from his father's boat while they fished each day in the sea. Because of the number of times Sean had seen Wheatgrass, he could actually recognize the young bird in the sky, and had taken to whistling to him as he flew by. Wheatgrass would always tip his wings and glide down near the boat while making his way to Devyn's cottage.

As Devyn shared the story of Eire with Sean, he felt deeply moved by what had happened and couldn't understand why someone like Eire would have married Dalbhach. It had to have been some spell that was placed on her family as well as the villagers and probably on Eire herself. From what he knew from Devyn, it seemed as if Eire was a very strong young woman who would not be easily tricked by such a man, and the proof was that she seemed to forget about Wheatgrass after he had fallen to the earth. Something about this was simply not right and Devyn agreed, but they knew that for now there was nothing that could be done. Even the people of Trefin had heard of Dalbhach. No one wanted to challenge him, or his raven.

***

More time passed and then one rainy day Sean was out in his boat with his father helping to pull in some fishing nets as they watched and worried about a serious change in the weather. The Irish Sea was a place that could be very dangerous if you weren't careful. Sean stopped working for a moment and looked into the sky. He noticed a seabird moving toward their boat. It was flying awkwardly, and it seemed that at any moment it might plunge into the water. Sean and his father let go of the nets and both watched the bird move toward them. Sean couldn't believe his eyes. Could it be? He grabbed a part of the net and held it skyward whistling and calling out Wheatgrass's name. The bird glided uncomfortably in their direction. With hardly any energy to spare, it landed in the net and struggled to gain its balance. It was Wheatgrass; after watching him fly by so many times, Sean would have recognized him anywhere.

Sean and his father could see that Wheatgrass had been injured. His body had scars that had healed over. His wings were fine, but it was obvious that he was still weak and recovering. It was possible that if he hadn't been able to land in the boat he wouldn't have made it to shore and could have drown.

They fed Wheatgrass some small bits of fish and put him in a fish cage that they kept onboard. Sean spoke to Wheatgrass trying to comfort him, and he noticed that the bird seemed to be paying very close attention to what he was saying. Wheatgrass settled down, ate some more of the fish, and rested quietly in the cage as they made their way back to shore.

5

Eire awoke in her beautiful bed at the top of Blackwater Castle. As she sat under the luscious red canopy, she gazed at the sun's rays glancing off of the huge paintings and bringing to life the colors on tapestries that covered the walls in her bedchamber. She had been in this room now for several months. If it had been just her bedchamber, it would have been a beautiful place to wake up, but it was more than that. It was her jail.

After the one time that Eire had tried to go home to see her family, Dalbhach had locked her in the top room of the castle and never allowed her out except when he wanted to show her off as his bride or sometimes when he traveled to celebrations where he was the center of attention. He seemed to treat her as his prize. He told her that he never wanted to lose her and that he loved her, but she did not feel loved. She felt watched by both Dalbhach and Rocas and knew that she had to constantly be on guard. He could turn on her at anytime, place a spell on her, and cage her back in her room. She treasured the few moments when she was allowed to be free, knowing that they would be very short-lived and that she would soon be back in her chamber at the top of the castle.

She spent many days wondering and thinking about her family, her village, her friend Devyn, and her wonderful friend, Wheatgrass. She knew that he had been killed, and every time she thought of him, a deep sadness passed through her. Yet, she still had some hope that he had somehow survived. Maybe he would come back to her. Maybe…

***

One night, Eire stood on her balcony gazing at the full moon. She spent a great deal of time on her balcony, as it was her way of experiencing some small amount of freedom. The view from her high perch atop the castle was breathtaking. She had an unobstructed view and could see a great distance across the green landscape, and on a clear day, she could look all the way to the sea.

Growing up, she had always loved the outdoors, and for so long now, had been denied the freedom to do as she wished. On those rare occasions when she was allowed outside the castle, Rocas was always flying overhead, always prepared to punish her with his claws or beak if she strayed too far or for too long. But the balcony of her chamber was a place where Rocas did not come. Dalbhach knew that he did not have to watch her there since it was so high and no one knew that she was there. There was only one other person, besides Dalbhach, whom Eire was able to see when she was in her bedchamber. That was Dalbhach's servant, who only came in and out to take care of his duties. She didn't even know his name, and he never looked at her. When he was there, Rocas was always at the door watching, making sure that nothing happened and that Eire didn't try to leave or talk to the servant.

That night the moon's light illuminated the landscape around Blackwater Castle in a beautiful, soft white glow that seemed to comfort Eire. It was a very clear, almost cloudless night, so as the pupils of her eyes adjusted, it was one of those times when she thought she could actually glimpse the Irish Sea in the distance. There was a mild breeze from the sea moving her hair, and she breathed in the night, feeling as if she were free for just a moment. Closing her eyes, she imagined herself being back near her home with her family. Growing up, she had spent many evenings near the sea, and she could picture herself there right now.

With eyes closed, her imagination firing, and her senses attuned to the night, her ears picked up a distant sound, a distinct high pitch that came and then faded away. She opened her eyes, letting her pupils adjust again to the moonlight and peered into the distance, trying to determine what she'd heard. It came again, only more quietly this time. She thought that it must have been moving away and not coming toward her. She listened a while longer and heard nothing. It had to have been her imagination.

She was about to turn to go back inside when she glimpsed the small black outline of a bird against the stark bright light of the moon. She watched with interest, thinking that possibly this was the source of the sound that she'd heard moments earlier. The bird gave the impression that it was circling, possibly peering down in search of something. Slowly, slowly the creature looked to be moving down, inching its way towards the earth. As it did, it appeared to be coming directly toward the castle. Eire watched carefully now.

Ever so cautiously, the bird soared and glided in a pattern that indicated an interest in Blackwater Castle, and even possibly in the balcony where Eire stood. She held her breath as she watched and noticed a familiarity of movement and form. Her memory began to tell her something that she dared not believe. Could it be? She continued to watch, and as the bird glided down and perched on the stone ledge of the balcony, Eire's heart jumped into her throat, tears came to her eyes, and she let out a muted squeal of joy! It was… It was Wheatgrass, her beloved Wheatgrass!

6

Over the next few months, Eire and Devyn wrote many times, as Wheatgrass traveled across the Irish Sea. However, that first message was by far the most wonderful, as she had not only learned that Wheatgrass was alive, but it had provided Eire with her first real connection in a long time with the world outside the castle. The notes were hers alone. Dalbhach could not touch them, and she valued them greatly and kept them safely hidden.

In that first note, she had learned how Sean and his father had saved Wheatgrass and how Devyn and Sean had helped him recover. She also learned that they were asking for her help in order to figure out a way to gain her escape from the castle and from Dalbhach. This frightened Erie because she knew how strong Dalbhach's powers were, and she worried greatly for her friends and for Wheatgrass. She didn't want to lose any of them or have any harm come to them on her account. She thought long and hard before she began giving them information to help with her escape. She decided to go forward for now, not really knowing for sure if she could actually escape. In fact, she doubted it, but somewhere deep inside she still had some hope and dreamed of a better life.

As the notes were traveling back and forth across the Irish Sea, so were many hand drawn pictures from Devyn. She was a wonderful artist, and she sent pictures of her family, some friends, and the man named Sean who had become such an important part of everything. Eire learned how he had always watched Wheatgrass pass over his boat in the early days before she had married Dalbhach. The pictures of Sean intrigued her. He was older than she and Devyn, but he was very handsome and had a look about him that calmed her.

Along with the pictures and descriptions that Devyn had given her, she began receiving messages from Sean as well as the ones from Devyn. He said that he'd seen a picture of her, as well, and had learned a lot about her from Devyn.

They, too, began writing back and forth. She was amazed at how caring he was. She felt a connection with him that helped give her strength and hope. She now had three friends working together to help give her back her life. Could it actually happen? She still wasn't sure.

***

The plan was beginning to come together, but it was becoming evident that someone was going to have to come and look the situation over in person and talk with Eire in order to finalize the details. It was decided that Sean would come, along with Wheatgrass.

Eire was nervous and frightened. She'd never met Sean, and she had been alone in her strange world for so long now that it was almost normal to feel isolated. The world outside seemed to be the fantasy. It was frightening to think of someone else coming into her world, but it was also very exciting. By now, she had not only reestablished her solid connection with her friend Devyn, but she had also made a very strong connection with Sean, even though she had never met him. She knew that he was someone that she could trust, and he had a joy about him that reminded her of when her life was once her own.

She agreed to allow him to come, and they determined that it would occur on the night of the next new moon. That way everything would happen in the very darkest of conditions. Eire was terrified!

***

The night came, and luckily Dalbhach was away that day. At least, Eire *thought* he was. She could never truly determine whether he was in the castle or not. She thought she'd seen him leave in his carriage earlier in the day, but he rarely communicated what he was doing. She knew that he did that as a way of keeping her off balance and controlling her. Also, she seldom knew Rocas's location or when he might show up in her chambers. He ordinarily only came when the servant was there, but even that didn't happen on a regular schedule. Everything was done so that she was kept off guard. Living this way created feelings of anxiety and anger inside Eire, and tonight she felt that anxiety very acutely.

Eire waited and waited, and watched and listened from inside her candle lit chamber. It was an eerily quiet night, and she was beginning to wonder if Wheatgrass and Sean would show up at all. Maybe she had misjudged the time somehow. This might possibly not even be the correct night. She sat on the edge of her bed and wondered.

It was getting later and later, and Eire was getting more and more tired by the minute. She lay back, and before she knew it, she was asleep and dreaming about Rocas tapping on her door with his beak. She woke up with a start. The candles were almost out. It was very dark, and she was groggy. However, she realized that the sound that she had heard was real and was coming from someone or something tapping on the door of her balcony. She picked up a candle and moved toward the sound, opened the door, and there was Wheatgrass with a small rope attached to one claw. The other claw had a note. She took the rope and note from Wheatgrass. It said that Sean was down below, and she needed to pull up the small rope, which was attached to a ladder made of fish net so that Sean could climb up. She gave Wheatgrass a little hug and pulled the ladder up. She secured it in her chamber. Her heart was pounding in her chest. She was very worried that Rocas might come at any second. Suddenly a hand grasped the ledge of her balcony, and a man hopped over and pulled the net ladder up behind him.

She held up the candle and looked at Sean. It was as if she'd seen him before. His eyes captivated her and felt like home to her. Her heart stopped, and she struggled to help him get the rope inside and shut the door to the balcony. They were together. Eire lit some new candles and asked Wheatgrass to go back out and watch for Rocas just in case, and he did.

***

The night was spent in an excited frenzy, discussing and planning the best way for Devyn, Wheatgrass, and Sean to help Eire escape from her chambers and begin her new life. They talked for hours, and Eire couldn't believe what a wonderful man Sean was. He had such an adventurous yet calm spirit. He was kind, and she knew that he was drawn to her and cared a great deal about what happened to her, even though he had only known her through Wheatgrass and Devyn and had only met her this very night.

Just an hour or so before dawn, most of the plan was finalized. Eire and Sean were both exhausted, but also elated at the possibility of getting Eire out of the castle for good.

They re-attached the net ladder for Sean's descent and then he turned to look at her. Eire couldn't help herself, she was so captivated by him, and they had spent such an incredible evening together. Before she knew it, Sean stepped toward her. He held her close for a moment, spoke reassuringly to her, their eyes locked, and she kissed him softly on the lips. It was an incredible night. She knew somehow that after that kiss, her life would never be the same.

***

After Sean had left, Eire, who had been caught up in the excitement of planning her escape and in the joy of meeting Sean, felt her loneliness creep back in as the dawn broke with a slight haze covering the sunrise. She walked out onto the balcony with memories of the amazing night filling her mind. Tears began falling down her cheeks. She felt very strange, sad, and frightened and wondered if she really had the right to involve these wonderful people in her predicament. Also, in a peculiar way, she was attached to this place. It had become her home, although it had been a very unhappy one. She closed the balcony doors, walked back to her bed, and cried herself to sleep with worry and doubt.

Could she really leave this place? Should she leave her husband, Dalbhach? Was her happiness worth risking the lives and safety of her dear friends?

7

The months of early spring passed. Eire had continued her existence in the tower with some outings here and there and evenings sitting with Dalbhach eating meals in silence. Since she had ceased any attempts to leave the castle, she was given more freedom by Dalbhach and was told that he would give her more and more independence as long as she behaved herself. Rocas, however, would still remain her constant companion, watching, observing, and keeping Dalbhach informed.

They also started going to more and more events together. They would make a grand entrance with Dalbhach introducing Eire to the leaders of each village. He expected her to smile and bow and then they would enter the gathering arm in arm as if she was the loving wife, and he the perfect husband. Rocas did not perform as often now. His job was to stay close, monitor Eire's movements and keep her from communicating with anyone in a way that Dalbhach didn't approve. It was wonderful to be out of the castle, but her life was still not her own. She carried a sadness and a level of fear, which made her miserable.

On one outing, she had felt more freedom in her movements as Dalbhach had allowed Rocas to perform for the crowd in one of the villages. She had walked over and started talking to a small child, almost forgetting where she was for a moment. As she did this, she immediately felt a cold, strong hand on her shoulder. The small child's eyes had frozen in place, and Dalbhach had kneeled down by her, whispering harshly in her ear, "What did you say to that child? Why were you talking to him? Were you talking about me or about the castle?"

Eire froze in terror. She tried to make Dalbhach understand that she was just asking the boy how old he was and if he had enjoyed the show. She could tell that Dalbhach didn't believe her. He told her that no matter what she'd said, the boy would not remember anything anyway. He motioned and Rocas came and walked back with Eire to the spot where she was allowed to stand to watch the proceedings. She noticed, as the small boy opened his eyes, that he shook his head for a moment and went back to playing with his friends as if nothing had happened.

Eire had experienced many such events over the past 2 years, some of which were more severe than others, but she never knew when they were going to happen or what Dalbhach would do. It kept her in a constant state of worry when she was out with him, and when she returned to the castle, he acted as if nothing had happened. He had controlled the situation, and he knew that he was all-powerful and still possessed his prize, the young Eire. She was escorted back to her tower by Rocas, and life went on.

***

It was now the middle of the summer. The fishing boats from Trefin and other villages traveled far and wide on the Irish Sea in search of the summer's catch of fish. Wheatgrass had made many trips back and forth to keep the communication going between Devyn, Sean, and Eire, and the plan for Eire's escape was almost ready. It would take place in about a week under the blanket of another dark night with a new moon.

Eire had done her best to discourage her friends out of fear, but they would not be deterred. The plan was going forward. Eire had begun to resign herself to that fact, but she was extremely agitated, worried, angry, and afraid. It was very hard for her to accept that her life and her happiness were worth that kind of risk. She had so many questions and very few answers, so all she could do, really, was go forward, and she did.

During these last few weeks, Dalbhach had started bringing Eire out of her chamber into his, almost every night. This worried her greatly. What if she was not in the tower the night that Wheatgrass, Sean, and Devyn were planning to come. She had to do something.

She thought and thought and decided to try to escape on her own. This way she would not risk the lives of her friends, and if anything happened, it would only happen to her.

So one night, as she lay by the sleeping Dalbhach, she carefully inched her way out of bed and moved toward the door. Rocas was nowhere around Dalbhach's chamber. She knew that Dalbhach didn't want him lurking anywhere near where he slept. She carefully opened the bedchamber door and moved quietly down the hall to another door that exited directly into the woods near the River Blackwater. Her plan was working. The only problem was that on this night there was still a slight sliver of the moon in the sky. It was just before the new moon when there would be total blackness, but she couldn't worry about that now.

Because of the small amount of light from the moon, Eire worked her way closer to the protective trees near the river. She bent down and drank some water. She was still very frightened, yet exhilarated, by the thought of being free. She began edging her way carefully along the water. Her eyes were now used to the light, and the sparkle of the small crescent moon on the water helped guide her. She knew the river, if followed, would go to a village downstream where she could hide and then decide what to do next.

She moved slowly, not wanting to make a sound, but as she stepped down, a small branch cracked beneath her feet. She froze where she was. She listened. She looked around. It seemed that she was still safe.

Just as she thought this, a huge lightning strike and roll of thunder lit up the night. Directly in front of her was the massive figure of Dalbhach with Rocas on his shoulder. The bright light behind him outlined his enormous, dark form. The lightning hit again and again and again, pounding into the mind of Eire till she lay unconscious on the ground at his feet.

He picked her up in his arms, and with Rocas leading the way, he soared up and up on the winds of the night to Eire's balcony. The door to her bedchamber opened slowly in front of him. He walked in, laid her on the bed, and placed an utterance upon her. She shuddered, took a long, deep breath, and then lay still. Dalbhach had finally taken absolute control of her. He would never allow her to wake again. He left her in a state that was halfway between being awake and sleeping. She was aware but unable to move or talk. He would keep her there forever.

***

After that night, Eire moved in and out of consciousness. She took to dreaming about herself as if she were awake and able to move. She was able to recognize the passage of time as the sun's rays and the shadows of the night passed by her window. She began to realize exactly where she was and what had happened, and she started worrying about her friends who would be there within the next night or two to help her escape. She understood then that her fears were well founded. There was no one more powerful than Dalbhach. She knew her friends were headed towards a fate much worse than hers. She had to worn them. She had to stop them. Her life was not worth the risk they were taking.

She struggled to emerge from her comatose state, but the struggle was useless. She felt all the emotions that had collected inside her for years now, but was helpless to do anything about them.

She knew that the night was almost upon her when Sean, Devyn, and Wheatgrass would come. It was still daylight. She had to do something. As she struggled with her dilemma, she heard the door opening. Someone was in the room with her. She couldn't tell who it was, but she could tell that it wasn't Dalbhach or Rocas.

She couldn't turn to look. Her eyes wouldn't open. A rough hand moved over her ear, and she could sense the coarse material from an old, tattered robe moving across her arm. She realized who it was. It was the servant. She had never really seen his face. The hood that he had worn had always covered it, and he wasn't allowed to look at her or talk. Even though this man was an enigma, Eire had always found him to have a quiet strength that she could see and feel.

She sensed his mouth next to her ear. He whispered something. She listened and couldn't quite grasp what he was saying, but he persisted. She was about to fade off into a deep sleep again when she seemed to finally understand. As she did, he was gone as quickly as he'd come, and Eire faded back into darkness.

8

Devyn and Sean had been traveling across the sea in Sean's boat. It was a blustery trip. Even though it was summer, a squall had passed over the Irish Sea and made their trip a little longer than they'd hoped. Because of this, they decided to send Wheatgrass ahead to check on Eire and let her know that they might be one night later than they had planned. Their arrival at Blackwater Castle probably wouldn't happen until the second night of the new moon. The good thing about the storm occurring was that they would probably have good weather and good seas on the return trip to Trefin.

Wheatgrass landed on Eire's balcony on the night that they had planned the escape. It was very dark. He pecked lightly on the door into her chamber and noticed that it was ajar. He squeezed through and hopped over to Eire's bed. The room was completely dark, not even a small candle was lit.

Eire could sense that it was nighttime and was in the stage of her constant stupor where she was somewhat more aware of things. She felt something on the bed as if it were hopping toward her. She knew almost immediately that it was probably Wheatgrass. He was now on her chest, turning his head back and forth looking into her closed eyes. He became more agitated and hopped up and down, pulled on her robe and pecked lightly against her cheek, but of course she couldn't open her eyes, couldn't talk to him, nor could she move. He stopped, finally, realizing that she could not respond. He turned quickly and flew as fast as he could out through the balcony door and back toward the sea.

Sean first noticed Wheatgrass as they were docking the boat near the shore. Devyn had gone into the village of Blackwater to find a place for them to rest for the night. They hadn't let anyone else know what they were doing, not even Eire's family. If things didn't turn out well, they didn't want anyone else involved.

When Wheatgrass landed there was not a note attached to his claw, which surprised Sean, and Wheatgrass was clicking his beak, scratching the ground, making noises, and moving very erratically and nervously. Sean knew immediately that something was wrong with Eire. He finished docking the boat, found Devyn, and they discussed what they should do.

As they talked, Wheatgrass became even more jumpy. They knew that something was seriously wrong, so they came up with a different plan and left immediately for the castle in the dark of night. They had to help Eire, and they had to get there as soon as possible.

***

The night passed and no one but Wheatgrass had been in Eire's room. She lay there wondering what was going on. She'd had visits from the servant and from Wheatgrass, but Devyn and Sean hadn't shown up as they had planned. In a way, she was relieved, although it all was very confusing, especially in her condition. All she could do was wait, lay there and wonder.

As the morning arrived, the servant had come in with Rocas. They had helped her stand and change her clothes. They'd fed her and placed her back on her bed, her body still limp and lifeless. Her existence had become so very strange. She even knew that Dalbhach had been there that day standing over her with his eyes cutting through the fog of her condition - his anger penetrating her very soul. This caused almost uncontrollable dread to pass through her, and then he left. She shuddered to think of what he might do to her friends if they came tonight to help her.

And… night did come, along with Devyn, Sean, and Wheatgrass. Sean tried to give Wheatgrass the small rope attached to the net ladder that they'd used last time to climb to Eire's balcony, but Wheatgrass shook his beak and refused to take it. It was what Sean was afraid of, but it was also something that he and Devyn had planned for. They'd shown Wheatgrass pictures that Devyn drew of different ways to get to the balcony. The one that Wheatgrass seemed to like best was to attach two large, strong fishhooks to the net and fly those up to the balcony. They didn't know exactly what Wheatgrass was going to do with them when he got there, but it looked like that's what they were going to have to try.

The hooks and the ladder were more bulky and heavier than the small rope had been and Wheatgrass was not a large bird. He grabbed the net ladder in his claws and started flying toward the tower. Devyn and Sean, hiding in the shadows, worried constantly as Wheatgrass flew slowly up the side of the castle with the ladder in tow determined to reach Eire's balcony. It was taking a long time, and they weren't sure that he could make it, but he did, and he hadn't been discovered.

In a short while, Wheatgrass returned, and the net ladder was lying against the side of the castle apparently secure and ready for Sean to climb up. If they could get Eire and leave, they had a carriage and two horses about a half-mile away securely tied to a tree. This would allow them to quickly flee back to their boat.

Sean began to climb. The net ladder slipped slightly and then tightened again, holding his weight. He moved up to Eire's balcony as swiftly as his strong arms would take him.

He jumped onto the balcony, opened the doors to Eire's chamber, and looked inside into the darkness. His eyes were already used to the black of night, but the room had even less light. He had to feel his way to where he remembered the bed was located.

When he found it, he almost immediately touched Eire's feet. She would have gasped if she could, but of course she could not move or make a sound. Sean had brought her out of being completely asleep to being somewhat aware. He could barely see the outline of her form now and noticed that she was not moving. He tried to wake her but was unsuccessful. He leaned over and could feel her breath on his cheek and hear her exhale softly. He wondered what had happened but knew that she could not get up and walk on her own. He decided that he was going to have to carry her and immediately wondered about the strength of the ladder.

He located one of her hooded robes nearby and did his best to put it over her shoulders. He wasn't succeeding. Her body was just too limp, so he balled it up and threw it down to

Devyn. Then he lifted her, placed her over his shoulder and walked to the balcony. Below, Wheatgrass noticed the ladder move and wanted to fly up to look, but Devyn signaled for him to wait. She didn't want him to go up and somehow be noticed. Wheatgrass paced on the ground below.

Sean's back and shoulder's were aching. His hands were slipping as the sweat was moving down his arms and dripping off his forehead. He held Eire over his shoulder confidently with one arm, but was worried about the hooks holding and about his hands slipping. Every rung of the ladder brought him closer to the ground, but it also put more pressure on the hooks that were the only thing holding the ladder firmly to the tower.

Finally, Wheatgrass couldn't stand it any longer and shot up the side of the castle. He passed Sean and Eire and noticed Sean struggling. Just then one of the hooks slipped, leaving just the one to anchor the ladder. They were about two-thirds of the way down. Wheatgrass flew onto the balcony and did whatever he could to keep the last hook in place. It slipped as well, but thankfully Sean and Eire were close enough to the ground that the fall was not harmful, and they, along with the net, landed in the grass at the bottom of the tower. Wheatgrass flew down and met everyone at the bottom. They were all relieved for the moment, happy to be together.

Amazingly, it seemed that neither Dalbhach nor Rocas had seen or heard them during the escape. Devyn and Sean held their breath and waited, but it seemed safe, and they proceeded through the darkness to the carriage. They covered Eire with the robe and then traveled the half-mile as fast as they could go with Sean carrying Eire and Wheatgrass watching over them from above.

They reached the carriage, untied the horses from the tree and placed Eire in the back. Devyn held her close while they proceeded back toward the boat, traveling slowly and quietly at first and then more swiftly under the cloak of a pitch-black Irish night.

Their plan was to not even stop in the village of Blackwater. They knew that was the first place where Dalbhach would look for Eire. Devyn and Sean continued on to Sean's boat with Eire, and Wheatgrass flew back and forth between the castle and his friends to make sure that no one had followed them. When everyone was safely on the boat, Wheatgrass landed and perched on the railing beside Eire. Now that she was safe, there was no other place that he wanted to be.

Dawn had just arrived, and the sun was rising over the village of Trefin on the other side of the Irish Sea. The weather was calm but with enough breeze to help their boat sail home in good time. It was a beautiful morning, and the danger of the night seemed to fade into the distance. However, Eire was still motionless, and although they had helped her escape, they wondered what Dalbhach had done to her and if she would ever be herself again. Devyn held Eire's head in her lap and cried and worried about her dear friend. She hadn't seen her for years now, and Eire lay pale and thin in her arms. Oh, what that horrible man had done to her. She hated Dalbhach and vowed to do everything she could to help bring Eire out of this evil trance. Wheatgrass sat on Eire's chest as Devyn was speaking and nestled down against her chin. Devyn watched this and could feel his sadness and how much he cared for Eire. He, too, would do anything for the person who had saved his life and been more than a friend to him. He loved Eire.

***

Sean was the first to notice land in the distance and knew that they had almost traveled the entire width of the sea. He could just barely see Trefin, his home, on the horizon. He had worked hard to sail the boat and bring everyone home safely, and now the dreadful thing that had happened to Eire had begun to weigh heavily on him as well. He couldn't believe that she might never speak, or walk, or laugh again; the tears began to well up in his eyes.

As he wiped the moisture from his cheeks, he noticed that the sky was beginning to change. It looked as if another squall was coming through. But how could that be? When he'd looked at the clouds that morning, he had been sure that they would have fair weather until they landed on shore.

The wind picked up. The dark clouds gathered, and the water started to become choppy and black. It didn't make sense. Wheatgrass noticed the change at the same moment as Sean. He lifted his head, stood, and took off like a shot into the sky. Sean and Devyn watched with alarm as he flew into the distance. Sean's attention was quickly diverted, though, as the wind was picking up strength, and he had to take down some of the sails so that they wouldn't tear or capsize the boat. They couldn't move forward at all now. They had to wait out the storm.

***

Throughout their journey, Eire had been aware of the events transpiring around her: the escape from the castle, the carriage ride, the boat crossing and the fear and worry of her friends as the storm raged about them. She was elated, frustrated, and extremely fearful. She could feel that things were turning badly. After all this time in Blackwater Castle with Dalbhach and Rocas, she could also sense when they were near, and she knew that her friends were in peril. Why had they done it? She knew that they were no match for Dalbhach, and she also knew that he would find her. She was terrified about what he might do to her friends before he took her back to that evil home. There had to be something that she could do. There had to be. But here she lie, with no movement in her limbs and not able to say or do anything to help. Fear and dread welled up inside her. She knew that Dalbhach and Rocas were on their way.

***

All around the boat, the sea was boiling now, and rain and lightning were pounding down from the sky. The sun was gone, and it was incredibly dark, except for the bright, ragged flashes of light piercing through and exploding on the black canvas all around. With each lightning strike, they could see and feel the threatening and foreboding thunderheads. Sean was busy securing the boat to make it as safe as possible while water sprayed up and over the sides of the craft from the brutal storm. Devyn was holding on tight to the boat and to Eire as seawater and rain gathered underneath them in the bottom of the boat, soaking through their clothes and into their bones. They could all feel the ominous danger of the moment and sense the evil that was approaching.

A violent bolt of lightning struck the mast. The wood splintered and broke off into the sea. Sean did his best to just hang on now. They were all at the mercy of the storm, helpless and consumed with dread.

Just as Sean thought their boat might be swamped, the wind calmed down, the lightning stopped, and the boat lay crippled and quiet under the sinister clouds created by the storm. Devyn and Sean looked at each other wondering if this might be the calm before the worst part of the storm. They knew this was Dalbhach's doing. They gazed skyward and saw a black spot hurtling in their direction. It became clear very quickly that it was the raven, Rocas. They crouched low to protect themselves, and Sean grabbed a gaffing hook to use against him. The bird continued to gather speed as it dove toward the boat. At the last moment, Rocas veered away from Sean and headed toward Devyn. She screamed and ducked just in time to escape the sharp claws of the huge bird. He gathered himself for another charge when out of the sky came Wheatgrass. He was flying toward Rocas at a speed that Sean had never seen before. Wheatgrass hit the large bird, and it seemed that the raven's wing was broken as he could hardly remain airborne. Wheatgrass flew hard towards the raven again to finish the job, but Rocas had obviously been faking the severe injury. He turned, and Wheatgrass flew directly into his claws. Rocas sunk his talons into Wheatgrass and landed on the broken mast with the small seabird locked in his claws and at his mercy.

Sean began to move toward Rocas with the gaffing hook. The bird didn't cower in the least and seemed to increase the pressure on Wheatgrass's body. Sean hesitated for just a moment, and as he did he felt as if someone was behind him. He turned and the massive figure of Dalbhach stood over him in black. His eyes were on fire, and the veins in his neck were bursting with rage.

Dalbhach lifted Sean and threw him into the sea several boat lengths from where he was standing. He then focused his attention on Devyn. His eyes slicing into her as she screamed in pain from the power of his gaze. She writhed on the deck with her hands held to her head. Rocas had let go of Wheatgrass. The small bird was unconscious from the blow and lay motionless on the deck. Eire sensed everything as Dalbhach walked toward her, and with a short incantation, she began to wake from the curse he had laid upon her. He wanted her to see with her own eyes what devastation she had caused by letting these people help her. He told her that he would make her watch, as he ignited the boat with his fury.

***

As the boat began to catch on fire, she looked straight into Dalbhach's eyes. She recognized the hideous wickedness that lay within him. She knew that if it wouldn't have been her that he'd taken as a bride, it would have been someone else, and because he was so incredibly powerful and controlling, he could have done this to anyone that had displeased him - anyone. He was pure evil! The anger grew inside her as she saw him for what he was, and as it did, her fear began to subside, and the night when the servant came into her room welled up in her mind. He had whispered something in her ear. What was it? What did he say? She knew it was important.

She was asking herself these questions when all of a sudden the great wizard held his neck on one side and then the other. Wheatgrass! It was Wheatgrass! He was attacking

Dalbhach with all his might, striking with claws and beak, as the raven looked on amazed. Wheatgrass was flying faster and with greater speed and agility than ever before. He violently struck and struck again, and as he did, Eire remembered what the servant had said. He said, "Fear is what imprisons you. Do not fear!"

Eire looked straight at Dalbhach and screamed at him, "I DO NOT FEAR YOU! I DO NOT FEAR YOU!" She ran at him and on her way she kicked the raven hard into the sea. She rushed Dalbhach, and for the first time ever, Eire saw fear in *his* eyes. He was being hit from all sides by the ferocious Wheatgrass and now Eire was pushing him, shoving him, hitting him, kicking him, and yelling her angry words in his face! "I DO NOT FEAR YOU!"

Dalbhach's body began to ooze blood onto his dark robes. He seemed to shrink in front of her eyes and hold himself against the onslaught of blows and words. Every wound that Wheatgrass created seemed to make him weaker, and every word that Eire said made him shrink from her. It went on and on as his power waned and fell away. The raven tried to crawl back onto the deck, but by then Sean had made it back to the boat and drowned the bird in the Irish Sea.

Devyn then, having recovered somewhat, rushed into the fray, helping Eire and Wheatgrass by pounding Dalbhach furiously with her fists and her screams until nothing was left on the wet deck except a bloodstained, mangled black cloak. At that very moment, the flames devouring the boat subsided, and the sun broke through the dark clouds, warming them from the cold of the angry sea.

***

Sean put out the remaining fires on the boat, and then sat with Eire and Devyn. They held each other close. Together they had worked and cared and fought for each other, and now at last, Eire was free.

Eire glanced up and watched as Wheatgrass hopped into her lap. All three of them smiled and reached out and touched him. They couldn't help but acknowledge the wonder of how courageous and loyal their remarkable small friend had been. As they all watched him, Wheatgrass quietly tilted his head and nestled down into Eire's lap. He seemed to enjoy the attention, and as they all had helped each other, he allowed them to help him as well.

When they were done cleaning and binding each other's wounds from the battle, they noticed some fishing boats nearby that were moving in their direction. They knew help would be there soon.

Eire couldn't believe what her friends had done for her. She would be forever in their debt, and together they had been able to get rid of a dangerous wizard that had been frightening people and using his evil powers in Ireland for many, many years.

They were all exhausted. They sat on the deck and talked and hugged and even smiled and laughed a little. Eire couldn't believe the feeling.

The sun continued to warm them, and the fishing boats had now surrounded them. Sean was helping his friends tie ropes onto his boat to haul it back to Trefin for repairs, and Devyn was gathering some food for them from the fisherman that came to help. Eire was simply too exhausted to do anything except sit with Wheatgrass in her lap. He was happy to be there as well, making short chirping noises and eating small bits of fish from Eire's hand. She looked down and smiled at him and told him how much she owed to him for all he had done. As she did this, he hopped off her lap and began scratching the wooden deck with his claws. She wondered what he was doing.

He finished scratching and hopped right back into her lap and cocked his head back and forth and pointed with his beak at the scratches. She leaned over and looked. It said, "I love you, Eire!" She gazed with wonder at her beloved Wheatgrass, tears glistening in her eyes, as she thought back to that day so long ago when she'd first found him in the wild Irish countryside near her home.

Made in the USA
San Bernardino, CA
01 December 2013